This edition published by Parragon Books Ltd in 2017

Parragon Books Ltd
Chartist House
15–17 Trim Street
Bath BA1 1HA, UK
www.parragon.com

Adapted by Emily Stead
Illustrated by the Disney Storybook Artists

Designed by Vanessa Mee
Production by Charlene Vaughan

ISBN 978-1-4748-7197-6

Printed in China

Bath · New York · Cologne · Melbourne · Delhi
Hong Kong · Shenzhen · Singapore

Lightning McQueen was a special race car. With a top speed of 200 miles per hour, he was fast. But speed alone does not win races. Lightning had to learn courage, loyalty and the value of friendship to become a true champion. Now he's the proud owner of seven Piston Cups.

It was the first race of the season at the Motor Speedway of the South. Lightning McQueen was leading the pack, ahead of his rivals, Cal Weathers and Bobby Swift.

All three cars stopped for new tyres, but Lightning came out of the pits the quickest to hold on to his lead. The three cars battled, it was a race to the finish. Then Lightning burned around the final bend to take the chequered flag. Ka-chow!

The next race in Arizona saw Lightning tear up the track, just as before. With one lap to go, this time McQueen and Swift were going head-to-head.

But as the flag came out, a slick black racer made his move. Jackson Storm zoomed past them both to take the victory.

"What a pleasure it is to finally beat you!" Storm teased Lightning after the race.

VROOM

Everyone was shocked that a rookie had beaten Lightning McQueen. In the TV studio, Natalie Certain and Chick Hicks looked back over the race.

"Jackson Storm is part of the next generation of high-tech racers. The racing world is changing, and Next Gens like Storm are taking advantage," Natalie explained.

"For the better if it means that my old pal Lightning is out for the count!" Chick Hicks chuckled.

The new season was about to get interesting.

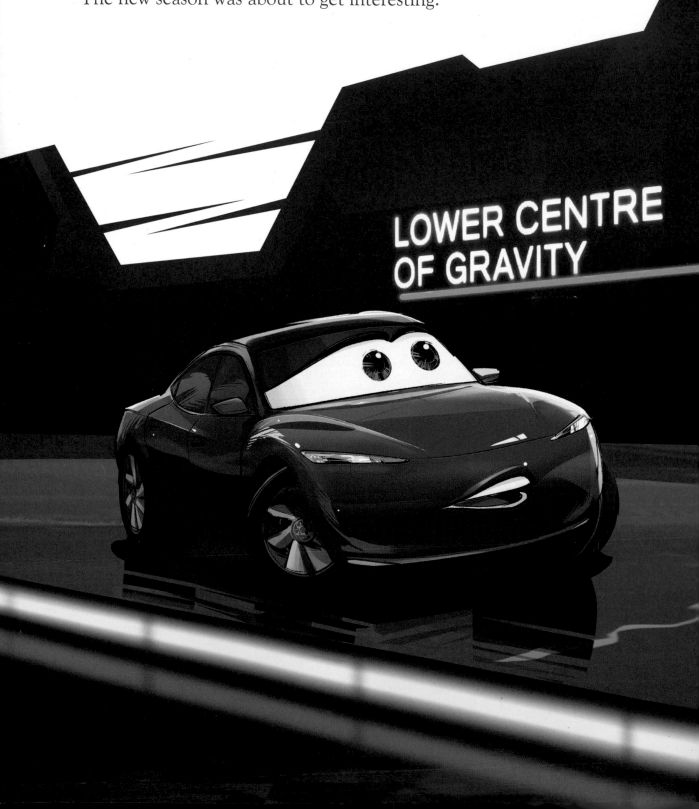

LOWER CENTRE OF GRAVITY

OPTIMIZED
DRIVE TRAIN

AERODYNAMIC
PROFILE

WIND TUNNEL SPEED **110** MPH

The next few races saw
Storm beat McQueen every time.
No matter how hard he revved his engine,
Lightning just couldn't keep up. His old friend Cal Weathers
retired and Brick Yardley was replaced by a Next Gen.

But Lightning wasn't about to give up – he loved racing too much.
By the time the last race of the season came around, Lightning had a
plan to beat Storm.

If Lightning made a steady start, he could save his speed to overtake
Storm in the final laps.

Lightning zoomed out of the pits with new tyres and plenty of fuel to take the lead. Lightning pushed as hard as he could, but Storm quickly caught up.

"Enjoy your retirement!" Storm laughed as he sped past Lightning.

Lightning pushed himself to the max until, suddenly, one of his tyres blew. His friends in the crowd gasped as he lost control, and went spinning across the track.

A terrified Lightning flipped into the air in a cloud of sparks and smoke. CRAASHH! At last, he skidded to a stop.

Lightning sat alone in Doc's garage in Radiator Springs. Months had passed since his big crash.

"Are Lightning McQueen's racing days really over?" the radio crackled.

Lightning sighed.

Then he watched a film of an old race – the one where the Fabulous Hudson Hornet had crashed. Doc Hudson had never raced again.

Sally and Mater visited Lightning to try to get him to train again. With his friends there to help, Lightning decided – he wasn't ready to quit just yet.

Lightning knew what he had to do. All his friends in Radiator Springs gathered round, as Lightning spoke to his Rust-eze sponsors. Dusty and Rusty had exciting news. They invited him to the brand-new Rust-eze Racing Centre, which had everything that Lightning needed to help him become a champion again.

After getting a cool new paint job from Ramone, Lightning rolled onto Mack's trailer, feeling great.

"Rust-eze Racing Centre, here we come!" Lightning smiled.

But when he arrived at the racing centre, there was
another surprise in store for Lightning. Rusty and Dusty
had sold the Rust-eze brand to a new sponsor! Sterling
was in charge now.

Sterling was a big Lightning McQueen fan, and had collected memories from some of Lightning's biggest wins. There were even some jars of dirt on display, taken from all the different Piston Cup tracks.

"Wow!" Lightning said.

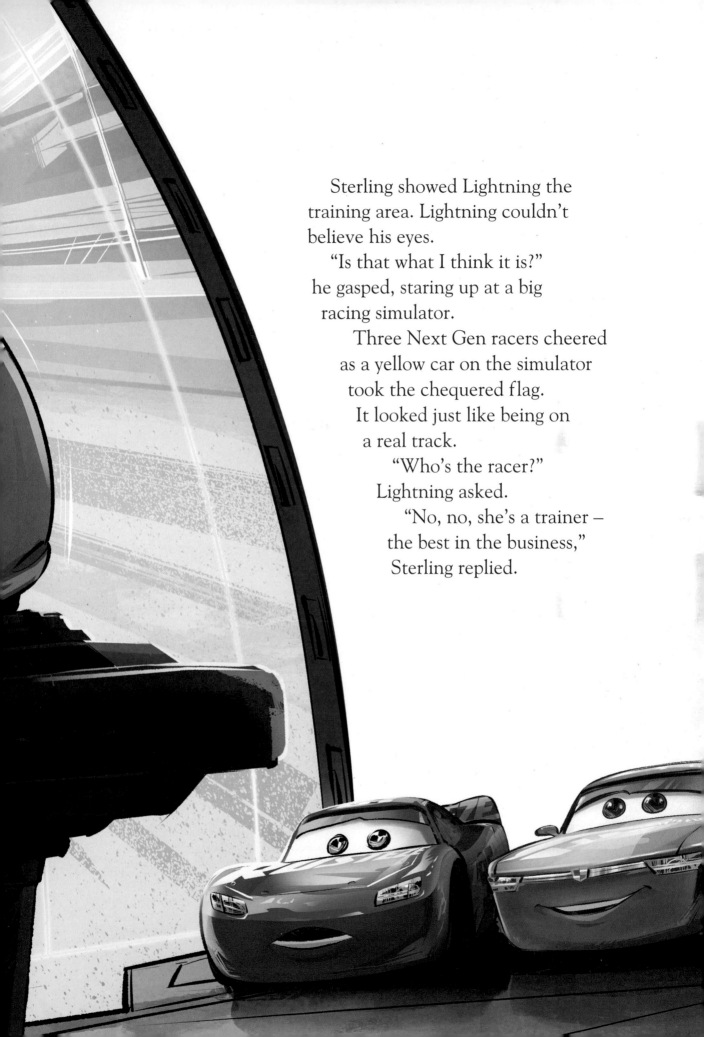

Sterling showed Lightning the
training area. Lightning couldn't
believe his eyes.

"Is that what I think it is?"
he gasped, staring up at a big
racing simulator.

Three Next Gen racers cheered
as a yellow car on the simulator
took the chequered flag.
It looked just like being on
a real track.

"Who's the racer?"
Lightning asked.

"No, no, she's a trainer –
the best in the business,"
Sterling replied.

The yellow car's name was Cruz Ramirez, and she was going to be Lightning's new trainer. All the young racers looked up to her. She was a cool and calm car who had great speed, too. Plus, she knew what to do to get the best out of her trainees. If anyone could help Lightning make a comeback, it would be Cruz.

Training began straight away with some simple exercises, but all Lightning wanted to do was to try the simulator.

Instead, Cruz made Lightning join the others on the treadmills. While the Next Gens zoomed along super-fast on their machines, Cruz had set Lightning's treadmill to just 5 miles an hour.

"We need to save your energy," she explained. "We'll work on your speed after your nap."

Lightning was not happy! But Cruz was right, Lightning felt much better after a short sleep.

When another racer rolled off the simulator, Lightning saw his chance. He sped away from Cruz and drove up the simulator ramp.

"How do I launch this thing?" Lightning wondered.

"Mr McQueen, wait until you can handle it!" Cruz called, chasing after him.

Sterling drove up to watch his star racer in action. But Lightning lost control, and crashed through the simulator screen!

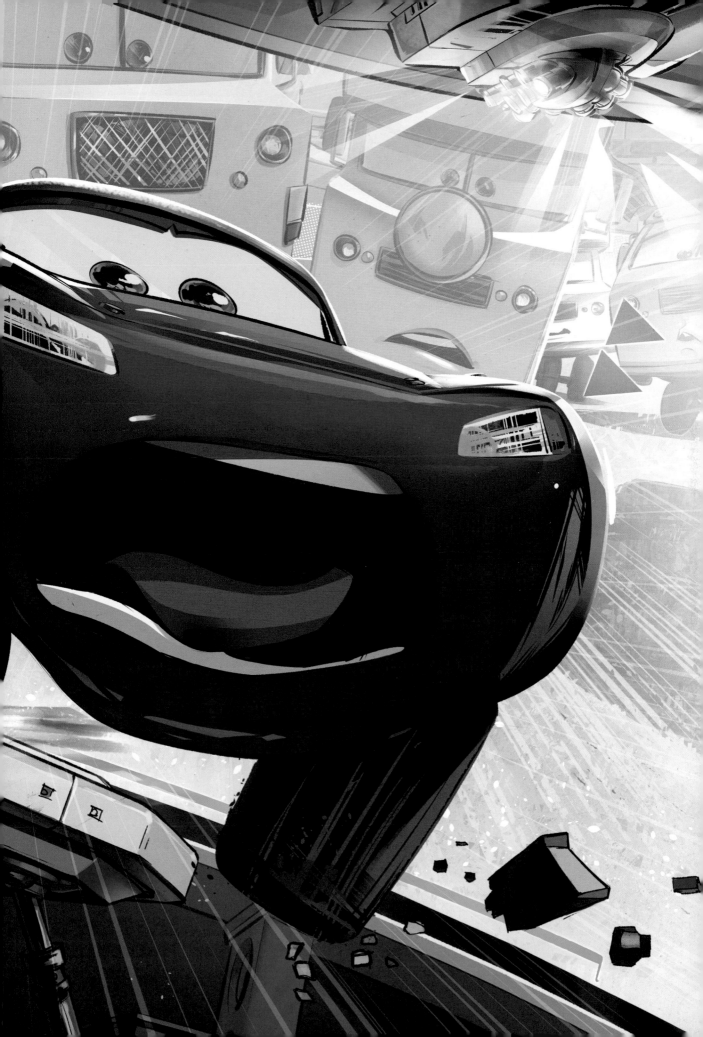

Cruz asked her boss to give Lightning a second chance,
but Sterling wanted to talk to Lightning alone. He called Lightning
into his office, which was packed with Lightning McQueen posters,
flags, cardboard cut-outs and even mud flaps.

Sterling told Lightning that he wanted him to give up racing and
get rich making movies and TV adverts instead.

"Racing is the reward," Lightning tried to explain. "I don't want to cash in." He begged Sterling to give him a chance to make a comeback.

Lightning was done with treadmills and simulators – he needed to train his own way and get his tyres dirty.

Sterling agreed that Lightning could go to Florida with Cruz to compete in the Florida 500, the first race of the Piston Cup season. But if Lightning didn't win, it was to be his last race.

Lightning and Cruz headed out onto Fireball Beach to start training.

Lightning raced to the pier at top speed.
Cruz had planned to drive alongside him to
track his speed, but she couldn't keep up
with him – her wheels just spun on the
soft sand!

Lightning tried to show Cruz what to do,
but she kept getting stuck. Then at last,
she tracked him all the way to the pier.
But Lightning's top speed was still slower
than Storm's.

Lightning needed to race against real racers. When he spotted a sign for the Thunder Hollow Speedway, he had an idea. He would race at the track there in disguise – he didn't want the cameras following his every move.

Soon, Mack's trailer was transformed into a party supplies truck, and Lightning was covered from bumper to bumper in mud.

His famous number 95 was now a muddy number 15. They rolled up to the speedway just as the race was starting.

Lightning introduced himself as 'Chester Whipplefilter'.
Then, to Lightning's surprise, Cruz drove up beside him.
She joined the race under the name 'Frances Beltline'.
Cruz was going to track Lightning's speed from the middle
of the stadium.

"Welcome to Thunder Hollow for tonight's C-raa-zyy
Eight!" the announcer boomed.

Lightning and Cruz looked at each other, scared, as stacks
of tyres exploded and cars began to smash into each other all
around them. This wasn't a normal race – it was a demolition
derby, and there was no escape.

"Make way for the undefeated champion, Miss Fritter!" the announcer roared, as a terrifying school bus thundered onto the track and charged towards Cruz.

Cruz couldn't move – she was frozen with fear. But Lightning spotted the danger and pushed Cruz to safety, just in time.

The action continued until a huge water tanker tipped over, spraying Lightning with water and washing away his muddy disguise.

"It's Lightning McQueen!" gasped a fan in the crowd.

After the race, Lightning was not impressed. None of Cruz's training had helped improve his speed.

"This is my last chance, Cruz!" he said angrily. "If you were a racer, you'd know what I'm talking about. But you're not."

"I wanted to become a racer forever," Cruz cried. "But the other racers were bigger and stronger – I didn't belong."

She wished him good luck, before speeding away back towards the Rust-eze Racing Centre.

Later inside Mack's trailer, Lightning couldn't sleep.
He decided to call Mater.

"Tell me what the problem is and we'll fix it," Mater smiled.

Lightning sighed. Doc could always fix Lightning's problems,
but he wasn't around to help any more.

"There was nobody smarter than old Doc," Mater agreed.
"Except for maybe whoever taught him."

That was it! Lightning had to find Doc's old crew chief – Smokey.

The next morning, Mack and Lightning headed for Thomasville –
Doc Hudson's hometown racetrack. On the way, they rolled up
alongside Cruz.

"Come with us," Lightning said to Cruz. "I'm sorry I yelled."

Cruz came on board, at last. Lightning told her about his plan to find
Smokey. They travelled on for miles, until Lightning spotted an old sign.

"Welcome to Thomasville, Home of the Fabulous Hudson Hornet,"
it read.

The old Thomasville track was no longer in operation, but it was still perfect for racing. Lightning and Cruz couldn't stop themselves from testing it out.

They whipped around the track. Lightning couldn't remember the last time he'd had so much fun. But as they skidded round the next bend, the cars had to brake hard. A figure stood before them on the track. It was Smokey!

"I know why you're here," Smokey said to Lightning. "You're thirsty."

Puzzled, Lightning and Cruz followed the old truck. Smokey introduced Lightning and Cruz to his friends: three racing legends who had competed with Doc, or 'Hud' as they called him.

Smokey told a story about a famous race, where Hud had flipped over the top of another racer in the home straight to take the victory! Cruz and Lightning were amazed.

Later on, Smokey and Lightning rolled outside.
"I need your help, Smokey," Lightning said.
They talked about Doc.
"Racing was the best part of his life," said Lightning.

Lightning didn't want to think that his own best years were behind him. Smokey smiled. He agreed that Hud had been sad after his big crash, but told Lightning that being his crew chief had made Hud happier than he had ever been.

"Racing wasn't the best part of his life – you were," Smokey said kindly.

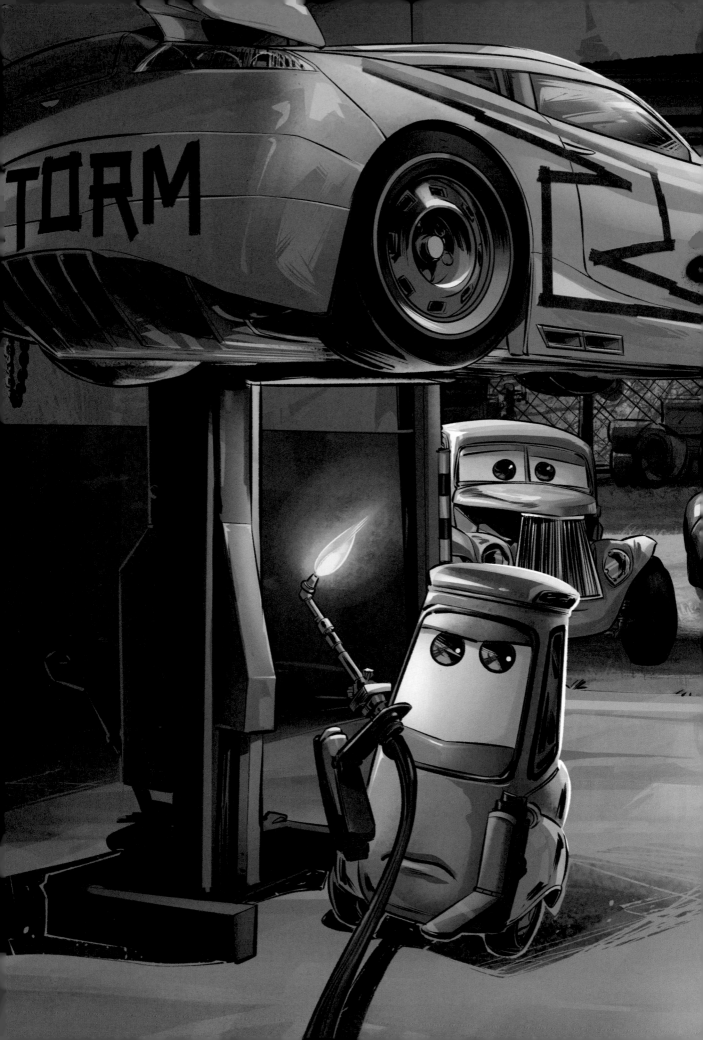

They headed back to the Thomasville track. Smokey had some wise words for Lightning.

"You'll never be as fast as Storm," he explained. "But you can be smarter than him."

To beat Jackson Storm, Lightning was going to need a training partner. So Guido and Luigi worked speedily, fitting racing tyres and a sporty spoiler to Cruz. They even taped 'Jackson Storm 2.0' to her side. Cruz was good to go. This time, though, as a racer, not a trainer.

Smokey gave Cruz a head
start of three laps. The racers took off
together, but Lightning couldn't catch Cruz.
There was work to do if Lightning was going to beat
the real Storm.

Smokey trained Lightning and Cruz hard. They pulled
heavy trailers, dodged bales of hay and even steered through
a stampede of tractors.

As they raced through a wood, Lightning's new wrap
tore away! The training was tough, but Lightning wasn't
about to give up – he was starting to feel like his old
self again.

There was time for one last race in Thomasville before they had
to head to Florida. Cruz had just a quarter-lap head start this time.
Lightning went out fast – he had never felt better. He pushed
hard around the bend, but it was Cruz who finished first.
Lightning crossed the finish line and slowed to a stop. He was
shocked. Even after all his hard work, he still wasn't fast enough.
Lightning was out of time – he needed to head to Florida.

The day of the Florida 500 race arrived. The stadium was packed full of fans, excited to watch a great day of racing. All the gang from Radiator Springs had come to cheer on Lightning. Smokey was there as Lightning's crew chief, and Cruz and Sterling were in the pits, too.

The racers were called to the grid. Lightning took a deep breath as he waited for the green flag to drop. He took off, and to everyone's surprise, number 95 made a strong start. Lightning pushed hard and began overtaking the racers in front.

Cruz tried to help, giving instructions to Smokey to pass on through his headset. But Sterling saw her, and ordered Cruz back to the racing centre.

"Take off those racing tyres," he told her. "You're a trainer, Cruz. Not a racer."

Lightning heard every word. As the race continued, all he could think about was Cruz: her speed on the simulator, all their races in training and how Cruz had beaten him every time.

Straight ahead, a car had smashed into the wall. Lightning swerved and headed immediately into the pits.

"I need Cruz back here!" Lightning told Smokey over his headset. He had realized that Cruz was a racer, after all.

A puzzled Cruz rolled into the pit lane. Guido, Luigi and Ramone worked quickly. When they had finished, Cruz had the number 95 painted on her side – Lightning's number. Lightning looked at Cruz proudly.

"Today's the day, Cruz. You're getting your shot," he told her. "I started the race, and you're gonna finish it."

As the race resumed, everyone was amazed to see a different number 95 on the track. The green flag dropped and they were off!

Cruz started slowly, but Lightning knew what to do. He asked Smokey for the headset, and took over as crew chief.

Lightning told Cruz to think back to their training, and imagine that Miss Fritter from the demolition derby was on her tail. Then he got her to remember the stampede of tractors in Thomasville.

Cruz imagined the cars as tractors, she looked for windows to steer around the other racers. The plan worked, and Cruz began overtaking the cars one by one!

"Go, go, go!" called Lightning.

With a lap to go, Cruz drew up alongside Storm. Storm was desperate to win – he wasn't about to let some rookie beat him. Cruz tried to pass on the outside, but Storm swerved hard, crushing her against a wall.

"You don't belong on this track!" Storm yelled.

"YES ... I ... DO!" she cried.

Remembering Doc's move, Cruz flipped up and over Storm.
She touched down again on the track in front of Storm, crossing
the finish line in first place.

The crowd went wild, and Lightning couldn't have been more proud of his friend.

Sterling interrupted the celebrations. "I could use you as a racer on our team," he said to Cruz.

"Sorry, Mr Sterling. I would never race for you," Cruz replied.

Instead, Cruz accepted an offer from Tex to race for Dinoco.

Then, Lightning and Cruz were announced as joint-winners. Lightning hadn't lost the race so he didn't have to retire!

No movies, no TV ads, Lightning had plenty of racing left in him yet, if that's what he wanted! Sterling left the stadium feeling almost as angry as Storm.

A few days later, Lightning and Cruz were back in training at Willys Butte. Cruz drove up in a Dinoco paint job, wearing Doc's old number 51.

Lightning had a new look, too. On his side read the words, "The Fabulous Lightning McQueen – Crew Chief." He knew his racing days weren't over, but for now, he was devoted to getting Cruz ready for her next big race.

It didn't matter who was the racer and who was the trainer – Lightning and Cruz were both true champions!